THE ● EARTH

Art Director: Rita Marshall
Book Design: Stephanie Blumenthal
Text Adapted and Edited from the French language by Kitty Benedict
Library of Congress Cataloging-in-Publication Data
Benedict, Kitty.
The earth/written by Andrienne Soutter-Perrot; adapted for the American reader
by Kitty Benedict; illustrated by Etienne Delessert.
Summary: A simple description of soil, including its physical makeup, and its
importance in maintaining life.
ISBN 1-56846-038-4
1. Soils—Juvenile literature. 2. Earth—Juvenile literature. [1. Soils.]
I. Soutter-Perrot, Andrienne. II. Delessert, Etienne, ill. III. Title.
S591.3.B46   1992
631.4--dc20   92-4551

THE EARTH

WRITTEN BY

ANDRIENNE SOUTTER-PERROT

ILLUSTRATED BY

ETIENNE DELESSERT

CREATIVE EDITIONS

In the country, a dirt path winds through the fields and forests.

The earth is packed down hard by the people, animals, and vehicles that pass along the path.

When it is hot and dry, the wind blows dust from the path into the air.

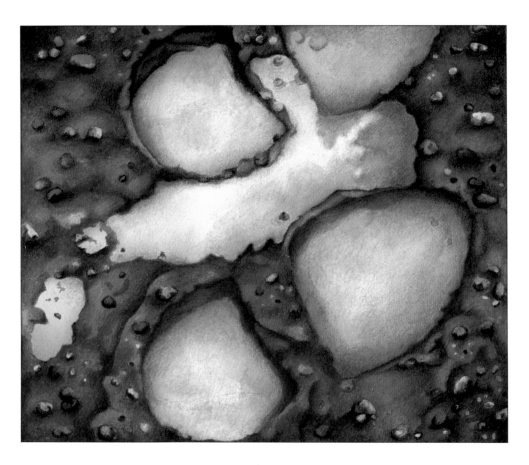

When it rains, the path becomes muddy, and footprints sink into the earth.

Mud and dust are both made of earth.

A farmer's field is also made of earth.

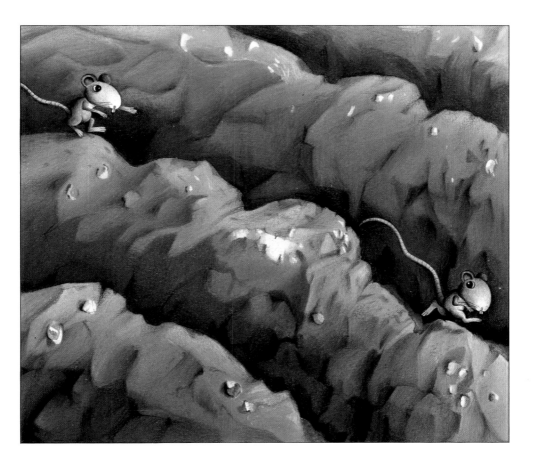

It is this earth, or soil, that a farmer plows in order to plant his seeds.

High up on the hillside, cows graze on the thick grass that grows
from the earth.

Nearby, birds nest in trees that have also grown from the earth.

The wind blows seeds from plants onto the earth, and the seeds settle into the soil and begin to grow.

Seeds need soil to grow. They cannot grow where the earth is covered with streets and buildings.

WHAT IS EARTH MADE OF?

In spring and summer, seeds grow into plants and trees, which grow leaves and bear fruit. The fruit swells and ripens.

In autumn, just before dying, the leaves turn red, yellow, and brown. When the leaves die the wind blows them to the ground.

The dead leaves become food for insects, small animals, and even some plants.

Rain makes the dead leaves soft. The leaves are then eaten by tiny plants called molds, and by even smaller organisms called bacteria. The dead leaves begin to decay.

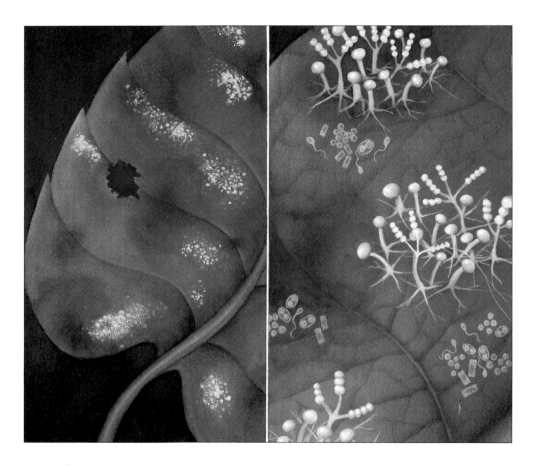

On the left, mold is growing on a dead leaf. On the right, the picture
has been enlarged so you can see bacteria growing. Bacteria are so
tiny that you cannot see them without a microscope.

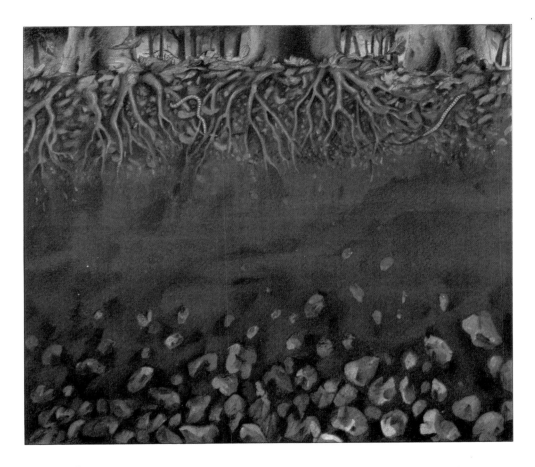

Within a few months, the leaves have disappeared. All that is left is a rich, dark powder called humus.

The humus mixes with dust, sand, small stones, and rainwater.

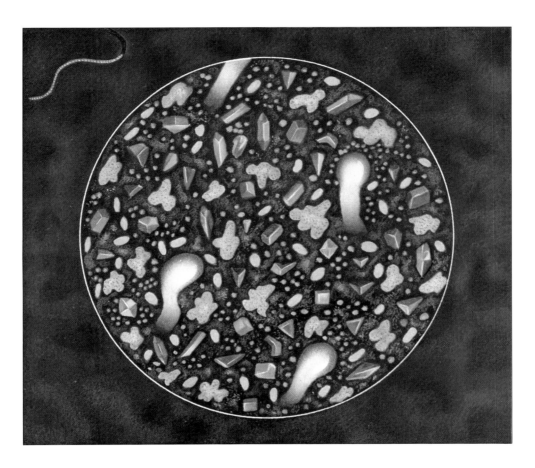

This mixture of humus, sand, water, and microscopic life makes up what we call soil.

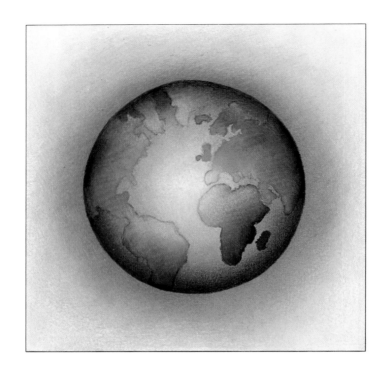

WHY DO WE NEED EARTH?

There are nine planets in our solar system.
The planet we live on is called the Earth.

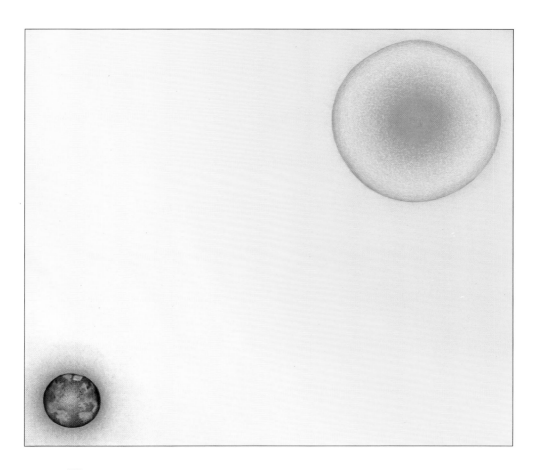

The Earth circles around the Sun, which gives us heat and light.

Oceans cover most of the Earth's surface.

The part of the Earth's surface that is above the water is called land.

The land is made of rocks, sand, and earth.

Plants need earth, water, sunshine, and air to grow.

Fish, animals, and insects need healthy plants in order to live.

In this way the earth supports not only our animal friends, but people as well.

Where there is earth, there is life.

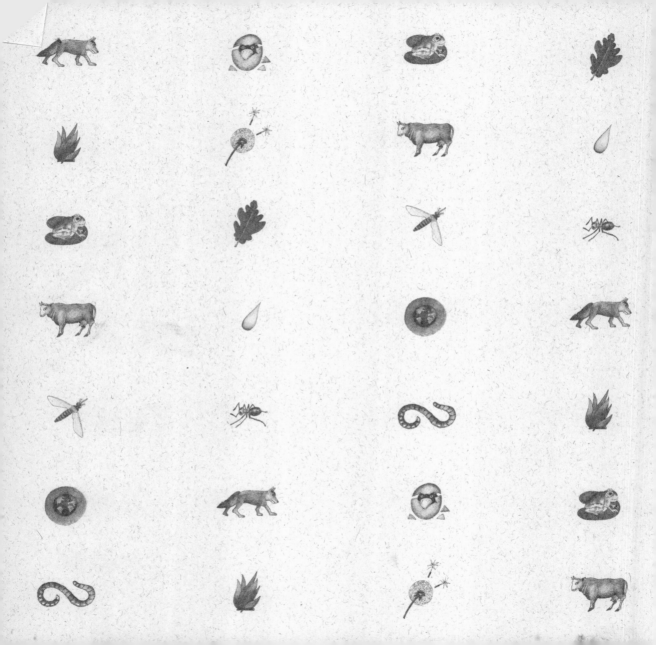